PEPPER
AND
ALL
THE
LEGS

BY DICK GACKENBACH

A CLARION BOOK • THE SEABURY PRESS • NEW YORK

For Gloria

The Seabury Press, 815 Second Avenue, New York, New York 10017

Copyright © 1978 by Dick Gackenbach

Printed in the United States of America.

LIBRARY OF CONGRESS CATALOGING IN PUBLICATION DATA

Gackenbach, Dick.   Pepper and all the legs.
"A Clarion book."
SUMMARY: Limited by his very short legs, Pepper the dachshund wonders what's upstairs—and finally finds out.
[1. Dogs—Fiction]   I. Title.
PZ7.G117Pe   [E]   78-5084   ISBN 0-8164-3221-X

Pepper, the dachshund, had very short legs.

They were so short that Pepper seldom saw anything face to face, except a mouse,

or a turtle,

or a mole in a hole.

Most of the time Pepper saw nothing but legs.

He chewed on big, fat table legs,

or curled up around stubby chair legs.

He played with legs in sneakers

and took long walks with legs in shoes.

When he was hungry, it was usually the legs
in sandals that fed him.

And every night,
Pepper was lifted
high above
all the legs
and given
a goodnight hug.

Then all his favorite legs
would climb the stairs
and disappear.

Where did they go?
Pepper wondered.
What could be at the top
of all those stairs?

No matter how hard he tried,
Pepper could never climb
those stairs.
His legs were just too short.

One day, Pepper saw a basket of clean wash.
And clean wash, Pepper knew, was always
taken upstairs.
If he couldn't climb the stairs, maybe he could get
someone to carry him there.
Pepper jumped inside the basket
and hid deep down
under the soft clean towels.

He waited until
someone carried
the basket
up the long, steep
flight of stairs.

When everything was quiet, Pepper came out
from beneath the wash.
He wagged his tail merrily as he began to discover
all the wonderful new things upstairs.

There were more legs, of course.
But there were also
new things to pull apart,

and new things to chew.

And new places to do things he should not do.

Soon Pepper found something grand and white.
He climbed on a stool
and down over the slippery wall.

The shiny knobs
sparkled
as Pepper began
to play with them.
Then,
WHOOSH!
The fun
was over
when the
cold water
poured out
on Pepper.

"YIPE, YIPE,"
called Pepper,
paddling as hard
as he could to stay
above the water.
"EEK," screamed
the sandals,
as they rushed
to pull Pepper
out of the tub.

"BAD DOG!" yelled the shoes.

"TSK, TSK," said the sneakers,
  when they dragged Pepper to the garage.

Pepper spent
the whole night
alone in
the dark garage.
No one hugged
him good night
and there was not
a leg of any sort
in sight.

But next morning
Pepper was forgiven and allowed
to return to the house.
"Now be a good dog," pleaded the sandals.
"Behave yourself," said the shoes.
"Please stay out of trouble,"
added the sneakers.

Pepper was very happy
to be back with all the legs.
He never tried
to climb the stairs again. . .

. . . but often
he dreamed
he had
great
long legs
that would
take him
anywhere
he wanted
to go.

Scobey, MT 59263